Milagro of the Spanish Bean Pot

Milagro
Spanish of the
Bean Pot

Emerita
Romero–Anderson

Illustrations by
Randall Pijoan

Texas Tech University Press

This book is typeset in Amasis. The paper used in this book meets the minimum
requirements of ANSI/NISO Z39.48-1992 (R1997). ∞

Designed by Kasey McBeath

Library of Congress Cataloging-in-Publication Data
Romero-Anderson, J. Emerita.
      Milagro of the spanish bean pot / Emerita Romero-Anderson ; [illustrations
by Randall Pijoan].
            p. cm.
      Summary: When eleven-year-old Raymundo, of Spanish colonial New
Mexico, overcomes his fear and asks a Native American woman to teach him to
make clay pots, his faith and hard work lead to a miracle that saves both of their
villages. Includes a glossary of Spanish terms.
      ISBN 978-0-89672-681-9 (lithocase : alk. paper)
[1. Indian pottery—Fiction. 2. Pottery—Fiction. 3. Droughts—Fiction. 4. Indians
of North America--New Mexico—Fiction. 5. Interpersonal relations—Fiction.
6. New Mexico—History—19th century—Fiction.] I. Pijoan, Randall. II. Title.
      PZ7.R66042Mil 2011
      [Fic]—dc22   2010046490

Printed in Korea
11   12   13   14   15   16   17   18   19   /   9   8   7   6   5   4   3   2   1

Texas Tech University Press
Box 41037 | Lubbock, Texas 79409-1037 USA
800.832.4042 | ttup@ttu.edu | www.ttupress.org

To my husband, Kent, and sister, Agnes, for taking the time to listen and help me every time I asked, and for traversing with me the creative wilderness of What if? Thank you.

Contents

Contents

Acknowledgments

Special thanks to all who assisted in the writing of this book: Charles Carillo for his research and book on a Spanish Colonial pottery tradition; our local genealogist Maria C. Martinez for writing about our ancestors in La Sierra; my mentor Mary Peace Finley for making me aware of this little-known but important slice of history; Mary Peace Finley, Maria Faulconer, Nancy Bentley, Carol Reinsma, and Denise Pomeraning, my Society of Children's Book Writers and Illustrators critique group for their invaluable critique and encouragement; my sisters Tish Herrera and Diana Cortez for reading the manuscript and giving me honest critiques; my sister Vikki Hinojos for reading it aloud so I could assess the pacing; my friend Randy Pijoan for his artistic brilliance in helping the story come to life; and my editor Judith Keeling and her staff at Texas Tech University Press, for their help and support in getting this book published.

Preface

This story, *Milagro of the Spanish Bean Pot*, gives us a peek into a time and place in history that is little known, but significant in helping tell America's story. Based on historical fact, there is ample evidence of a Spanish Colonial pottery tradition from about 1790 to 1890 in northern New Mexico and southern Colorado. Some archaeologists would argue that only Native Americans made clay pots.

Milagro
Spanish *of the*
Bean Pot

One
In Search of a Miracle

The high-pitched call of crows triggered the unwanted memory. Caw! Caw! Caw! What was once a familiar sound turned to a stabbing pain in Raymundo's chest. He was tempted to turn and run the other way, disappearing forever into the hot September day. He had never felt more alone—except for the day his life changed forever.

That morning, he had been on his way back from the plaza. Papá sent him home for the hoe he'd fixed and forgotten. He could see the crows that nested on the trees along the river taking flight, scattering like ashes in the wind, announcing their departure with piercing cries. Something had spooked them.

Raymundo ran up the hill to see what it was. Dropping to the ground at the top, he lay flat on his belly. He would never forget the sound of thundering hooves and shrill yelps down below. Comanches zigzagged around the field, tearing out bean plants and slinging them over their horses' backs.

Papá! Where was he? Raymundo squinted, desperately looking for Papá, but a thick cloud of dust blurred everything. More than anything, he wanted to go look for his father, but knew it would get him killed.

Then the raiders rode away, the echo of their voices fading to a whisper.

A gust of wind kicked up, sending Papá's hat rolling out of the dust cloud. Raymundo jumped up and ran down the hill, expecting his father to walk out of the cloud, too.

The air cleared. Papá lay on the ground, the dark wet splotch around his head spreading like a halo, growing larger the closer Raymundo got.

That had been almost a year ago today.

Now, Raymundo stood at the edge of the bean field. He had not run away like he wanted to when things got hard. He knew what Papá would have expected. But he didn't know if he could always measure up.

Planting a field of *bolita* beans had tested him. Without Papá, Raymundo had pulled the handmade plow like a draft animal. He planted the family's two hundred *varas* of bottom-land, keeping with the agreement of the Spanish land grant. Mamá would not lose the land, and the bean crop should keep them from starving this winter

Every day, he watered the plants he was trying to save from the drought and guarded them to keep out enemies. He never knew when the Comanches might return.

Today, however, like every other day this season, the enemy was drought. And birds. The birds he could do something

4

about. "Shoo!" he shouted, throwing rocks at a squadron of noisy crows.

Raymundo filled a clay jar with muddy water from the trickle in the old *acequia*, the irrigation ditch he had burned clean of dead willows in early spring. Taking small steps so the water wouldn't spill, he poured it in the little crater of a bean plant. He picked up a handful of dead leaves that had dropped off the rows of thirsty plants getting no water and crumpled them with his fingers. He knew that when all the leaves were gone, the plants would stop growing.

He finished watering the small patch of beans he'd sectioned off, hugged the water jar to his chest, and removed Papá's hat. "Thank you, Papá, for teaching me to plant," he said, as if Papá were standing beside him. He patted the clay jar. "And thank you, little *tinaja*, for helping me bring water to my plants."

The fierce sun had baked Raymundo's skin the color of cocoa beans. His dark eyes matched the color of his hair, which absorbed the sun's heat and burned his tender scalp. Clouds were forming to the east, but it wouldn't rain. Every day he watched the clouds evaporate into a hazy mist.

"I can do nothing more here, Papá," he said. He wiped his brow, took a drink from his water skin, and put on Papá's hat. "I will return later to check on my plants." He hid the hoe under the dry sagebrush he placed around his bean patch every day to protect them, and walked home.

Raymundo approached the tiny Spanish Colonial village where Papá and Mamá had settled with a small group of neighbors they called *los vecinos*. He entered the sturdy plaza gate and walked past dusty, red adobe houses that joined to form a square. Scraggly goats and sheep looked out from pole and brush corrals toward the back. Piles of broken clayware littered the sides of doorways. *Vecino* Juan, the village moccasin maker, was using one of these shards to scoop out ashes from the *horno*, an outdoor oven made of adobe brick.

"*Buenos días*, Señor," said Raymundo before entering his family's quarters, a single room for him and Mamá.

Mamá was cooking lentils in the shepherd's hearth in an *olla de barro*, a clay pot. She wiped away tears with the corner of her apron.

"Why are you crying, Mamá?" asked Raymundo. He set his water jar on the ledge of the hearth, which extended along the wall and served as his bed.

"Our only bean pot is cracked," she replied. Raymundo's eyes followed a spurt of water running down the side of the pot. Puffs of steam rose from the hot stone trivet. She wrung her small, chapped hands. "What will we cook in? I know nothing about making pots of clay."

"Do not worry, Mamá. I will find a way to mend the pot. And if God wills, we will have beans at harvest to cook in it."

He guided Mamá to the wool-filled mattress on the *tarima*, an adobe bench attached to the wall and low to the floor. "You rest. When Tía Clotilde arrives, she will do the cooking and cleaning. I will gather wood and tend the bean field. We will be all right. You'll see."

Raymundo sounded more sure than he felt. He didn't know

how to patch a clay pot. And what if the river dried up completely? They would have no food to cook in the pot, even if he could mend it.

While Mamá slept, he took his rosary and the little velvet-covered casket from under his pillow on the hearth ledge. Papá had traded two serapes for it in Chihuahua, and Raymundo kept it safe for the family's use. The leather-hinged lid opened upward and inside lay little silver images called *milagros*. He took the image of a woman and pinned it to the cloth vestments on the wood-carved *santo* of Saint Anthony on the mantle of the hearth. He fingered the wooden beads on his rosary and whispered prayers to the saint of miracles, to restore his mother's failing health. The silver *milagro* would help bring the needed miracle. If only there was an image for a clay pot, he could ask for a blessing.

Two

Clay Woman

After his daily prayers, Raymundo shouldered the cloth wood-sling, refilled his water skin, and walked the short path toward the sloped mesa up ahead. His search for firewood took him to the crest, past the small village of *genízaros*, a group of Indians who were ransomed from captivity to the Spaniards. They were given land here far away from the capital and Spanish society before Raymundo was born.

He could see their houses through spaces in the fence made of thin crooked poles held upright by woven willow branches—three adobe houses red as the hills and two made of stone.

The pot maker, Clay Woman, sat on a goat skin in the patio of a small adobe house. She stood out, as did the village medicine man, for they alone wore traditional dress. The other genízaros wore the shirts, trousers, dresses, and skirts of the Spanish Colonials.

Even after *los vecinos* suspected that Clay Woman was a witch, Papá had traded a weaving for one of her bean pots. Raymundo understood Papá did not hold that belief, and chose to try and understand her and her people. When Clay Woman walked past the village carrying her cloth sacks, Papá had asked the others to allow her passage without bother, but now he was gone, and things were different.

Was Clay Woman working with clay? He couldn't tell for sure. Leaving the path, he crouched behind the large bushy *chamiso* hugging the corner of the fence. The search for wood would have to wait.

Raw clay and molded pots dried on a faded rug in the hot sun. Several finished pots were set against the trunk of a cottonwood.

If only he could have traded for a bean pot.

Clay Woman had a fire burning in a pit, and a beautifully shaped pot rested on large stones in the shade. The old crone's hair looked like a magpie's nest. She wore a manta wrapped around her body and held together with a long belt at the waist. Her feet were bare. He saw that her hands were big as she sanded the surface of the pot with a lump of rough sandstone.

The medicine man, Fools Crow, sat close by, eating something wrapped in a corn tortilla. His hair was matted and filthy, hanging long on the back and sides. Grime caked like mud plaster on his skinny torso. He was covered from the waist down in leather leggings, and a large pouch hung from his shoulder. Raymundo knew he didn't live here with the others,

11

for he heard Fools Crow's mysterious songs while working in the family bean field.

Fools Crow leaned and said something to Clay Woman. He looked briefly in Raymundo's direction and shivers raised the hairs on Raymundo's neck. Then he heard it. The unmistakable sound of the snake's rattle, not unlike the rattle a shaman uses to scare away meddlesome invisibles. His senses warned him—DON'T MOVE!

Raymundo moved only his eyes, his heart beat in double-time. He heard the roar of blood rush around in his head, and sweat poured out of every pore in his body.

The venom of a rattlesnake kills.

From his crouched position, he saw that Clay Woman was alone now. Fools Crow had disappeared.

The muscles on his legs cramped. Unable to hold himself up, he slumped and waited for the snake to strike. Seconds ticked by. He finally dared look behind him. Raymundo stifled a scream when he realized what he was seeing was a twisted twig. No slither tracks in the dust, nothing. Was he so afraid of spying like this that his mind played a trick on him?

I heard the rattle, he told himself.

Shaken, Raymundo slowly stretched his muscles. He wanted to leave this place and never come back, but was drawn to Clay Woman once more. He watched in fascination as she coated her pot with a watered-down white clay paint using a small cloth mop. As soon as one coat dried, she added another until she had an even color. Then she began to polish it with a smooth river stone, switching stones to fit a curve, the base, or an edge of the pot. She rubbed the surface again and again.

Could he do what Clay Woman did and mend their bean pot? He had to try.

Raymundo backtracked to the path, ruminating as he walked. He heard the snake rattle over and over in his mind.

He found a few sticks for the evening fire, then walked to the far end of the bean field, to the barro pit where he and Papá used to make adobe bricks. A seam of clay was embedded in the eroded layers of a dry wash. It had once belonged to the ancestors of a Tewa Indian pueblo, Papá had said, but the native people were no longer allowed on land granted to the Spaniards by the Spanish Crown in the Kingdom of New Mexico.

He wondered where Clay Woman got her clay.

Scooping two handfuls of clumpy reddish-brown clay, he dropped it in the wood-sling. He found a smooth stone by the river bank, put it with the clay and began the walk home, taking care not to spill his load.

Tía Clotilde met him at the door. A bulky skirt billowed out from her plump hips and filled the doorway. She wore a little sleeveless coat over her fancy blouse, her hair held tightly in a bun.

"Hola, Tía. We're so happy you came to stay. Aren't we, Mamá?" He kissed Tía Clotilde's chubby cheek.

"I was lucky Padre Sanchez had a baptism. However, he managed to bore me with his constant prattle. He talks more than I do, if you can believe that," she said, hugging him. "So you are man of the house now." Tía Clotilde held him at arm's length.

"And only eleven years," said Mamá from her bed. "Papá would be so proud."

"No more women's work for you," said Tía Clotilde, handing him some sticks. "Leave that to me." She dipped her hand in a shallow wooden bowl to sprinkle the dirt floor before she swept. The ox blood, wood ash, and straw that made it durable had worn off, and the floor gave off dust.

"No, Tía. We cannot spare water," said Raymundo.

She swept anyway, her broom's long-stemmed grasses skimming the floor, filling the room with a fine dust that choked Raymundo and Mamá and made them sneeze.

Raymundo opened the door to let the dust out. Then he built a cook fire in the hearth. "How are you feeling, Mamá?"

"I am so tired," she said, sniffling. The sagging skin on her cheeks made her look older than her years.

"She needs to eat to regain her strength," said Tía Clotilde. "But how can I cook a meal?" she said, holding up the cracked bean pot. "Why have you not traded for a new one?"

"The genízaros no longer trade with us," said Mamá. "They send their pots south on the Camino Real, the Royal Road to the markets in Chihuahua."

"And who are they, not to trade their pots. Neither Spaniard, nor Indian for that matter, since their own people won't take them in."

"It is the only way they know," said Raymundo.

"Evil *brujos* is what they are. Won't trade their pots, indeed."

Were Clay Woman and Fools Crow really witches with the power to shape-shift into birds and animals or skinwalkers as the storytellers claimed?

"Don't go near them," said Tía Clotilde. She looked at Mamá. "Remember what happened to Father Ordóñez? I believe the year was 1796. I had come for a visit and that's all everyone talked about. The genízaro witches put a curse on him, Raymundo, and he died a terrible death."

Raymundo had heard the story many times. The priest's stomach had bloated like a cow's after eating too much green alfalfa. He couldn't sleep, yet was unable to leave his bed. His veins swelled so that he vomited blood and bled through the nose.

The power of a curse could destroy the peace of a village for years to come, Raymundo knew. Several people had died that year. He himself had been robbed of an older brother, and according to Papá, Mamá had never been the same.

"Here, Tía," Raymundo said, taking the cracked pot. "I will try to mend it later."

Tía Clotilde filled two wooden dishes with *tasajos*, strips of dried pumpkin. She handed one dish to him and one to Mamá, who nibbled only a few.

After supper, Raymundo ground the clumps of clay on the same stone *metate* they used for grinding corn. He added water to the powder. Instead of a cloth mop, he used the palm of

15

his hand to slather the moist clay over the crack on the bean pot, the way Mamá mud-plastered adobe walls. He brushed away loose clay, then polished and sealed the surface over and over again with the river stone.

Before he went to bed, he made a little clay milagro in the shape of a bean pot. He placed it on the mantle along with Mamá's image on Saint Anthony's cloak. Again, he prayed for a miracle—for Mamá's health *and* for the mending on the bean pot to hold.

Saint Anthony would hear him and answer his prayers.

Three
Down the Royal Road

Raymundo awoke to his aunt's chatter. "It will be even hotter today," said Tía Clotilde, fanning herself with her hand. "It is already too hot in the house." She picked up the bean pot. "Now, let's see if your patch works, *mi amor.*"

He held his breath as she poured in a cup of water to cook *atole*, a blue cornmeal mush. No leaks. At least not yet. He signed a cross on his forehead.

"Our little man has done well," said Tía Clotilde, patting his back. "As you know, no other pot will do, for only a clay pot gives beans that heavenly taste. We will have to take special care with this one, since we can't trade for another."

He sat on the woven rug by the hearth and ate his breakfast while Tía Clotilde chattered.

"I hear you have a bean crop."

Gulping the last bite, Raymundo stood, shouldered his water skin, and reached for his jar. "Yes, and I had better hurry

and water, or we will lose it in this heat," he said on his way
out the door. He would have to get used to another person in
the house. Especially one who talked so much.

At the bean field, he walked back and forth to the ditch, watering each bean plant. Brown leaves from the rows of dying
plants swirled around in little dust devils caused by the stifling
wind. "We need rain soon, Papá."

Raymundo finished watering and trod the path to the
genízaro village again, veering to stand closer to the fence.
Clay Woman was at work. Beautiful ocher-colored designs appeared on the white pot with each stroke of her yucca brush.

A boy about Raymundo's age walked up and spoke to Clay
Woman. "The vendor comes," he told her, and ran off. Ray-
mundo had understood, for the boy spoke a form of simple
Spanish.

Raymundo cringed at the shrill squeak of the ox-driven
cart. The wheels were made of cottonwood trunk with a
pine-wood axle on which rested the cart bed. The merchant
was here to collect the finished pottery. The cart was heav-
ily loaded with trade merchandise that poked through spaces
between slender branches lashed upright. He made room for
the pots among buffalo and deer hides, weavings, and blan-
kets. The oxen chained to the yoke strained to pull the wagon
through the village gate.

Again, there would be no pots left to trade with los vecinos.
No pot for Raymundo—even if he'd had something to trade.

Raymundo slipped away unseen. He ran home. His face

felt hot and his head began to pound. Good, Mamá was asleep and wouldn't see him if he cried. And Tía Clotilde? Was she quilting and gossiping with *vecina* Ana next door while Mamá slept? She lived for gossip.

Raymundo sat at the loom where Papá had woven the serapes he sent south for those who could afford to pay. He fingered the pottery shard Papá used for a drop spindle. "If we had wool, Papá, I could learn to weave and trade for what we need," he whispered, a lump in his throat. "If only I could make adobe bricks to sell, like you and I did every summer. But for that, I would need plenty of water."

Mamá stirred, and Raymundo pulled himself together. "How would you like to sit outside for a while?" he asked. Maybe it would take his mind off his worries.

He sat with her in the patio. It was early afternoon, and the turquoise sky gave off strong heat from bright sunlight. A rosy blush tinged Mamá's pale cheeks.

Three boys played *chueco*, an ancient game of the Pueblo Indians, a game of great skill that Raymundo loved. He sat there brooding, planning strategy in his mind. He ached to be out there, running with the curved stick, dribbling the rawhide ball down the long playing field.

"Go, *mi'hito*. Join them," said Mamá.

Play? It had been so long since he'd had the time. He looked at Mamá.

"Go on," she said again.

He kissed the top of her head and went to join the boys.

Raymundo ran and ran, advancing the ball every time it was his turn, scoring points for his team. He ran and stole the ball several times, and he ran just for the joy of it.

Raymundo stopped to rest. He idly watched vecino Juan's young daughter run to the gate after her little dog. The dog stopped and barked. Juan dashed out of his house and scooped up his daughter. "Go away," he shouted. "You don't belong here."

Raymundo glanced out the opened gate. Clay Woman carrying her cloth sacks waddled past and looked in. Her eyes lingered on Mamá.

A look of terror transformed Mamá's face. "A genízara witch!" she cried.

"What are you looking at, *bruja*?" shouted a boy. He ran to the gate and picked up a stone to throw at Clay Woman.

"Hey, Tomás, leave her alone!" shouted Raymundo, running toward Mamá.

The boy dropped the stone and ran off slinging hateful words instead. "Skinwalker! Skinwalker!" he chanted.

"Ay, *Dios mio*," whispered Mamá. She made a sign of the cross on her forehead, her lips, and over her heart.

"Do not be afraid, Mamá. She won't hurt you," he said, thinking of the beauty Clay Woman created with her hands. How could she be a witch?

Tía Clotilde walked up, a paper of pins dangling from the bodice of her fancy yellow dress. "What is the matter?" She helped Mamá up.

21

"She's ready to go in, Tía," said Raymundo. "I have to go now, Mamá. Try to rest."

He hurried out the plaza gate, hoping to catch up with Clay Woman. Where does she go with those sacks? He wanted to know.

Raymundo followed Clay Woman a long way down the dusty path toward the distant mesa. Every so often, when she'd stop to catch her breath, he'd hide behind the low-lying sage and piñon pines. Finally, she came to an arroyo, a dry gully cut into the side of the mesa. A clay bed with seams of rainbow-colored clays layered the bank.

So this is why she came so far . . . to collect clay, marveled Raymundo.

After filling the sacks, Clay Woman dragged them along the path. Suddenly, she stopped, clutched her chest and wavered.

The heat! Is it making her sick? Raymundo started to run to her, but Clay Woman steadied and went on her way. He walked far behind toward home.

He stopped at the bean field. Using the wooden hoe, he removed weeds so they wouldn't strangle the plants, but the plants looked wilted even after he watered them for the second time today. It was nightfall before he was done.

Raymundo's stomach growled. Would there be something to eat when he got home? Mamá was getting more frail every day. He, too, must eat to keep up his strength, but their food supply was dwindling fast with one more mouth to feed. Mamá and Tía Clotilde would not make it through a drought year without him.

While crossing the plaza, Raymundo heard a group of men talking in angry voices by the well in the center of the village patio. He couldn't make out faces in the dark. It sounded like vecino Juan. "The genízara, Clay Woman . . . ," he began, but quit when he saw Raymundo walk by.

What was Juan up to?

four

A Skinwalker's Moon

The faint aroma of soup cooking greeted Raymundo as he entered the house. Tía Clotilde had managed to scrape together half a cup of split peas to cook in the patched bean pot. A hair-like seam of moisture began to show along the edge of the crack, but still no leaks.

Tía Clotilde's snoring kept Raymundo awake far into the night. Thoughts of making clay pots churned in his head. Suddenly, there arose in him a fear of starvation so great it threatened to choke him. For without the bean pot, there was nothing to cook in. Iron pots were scarce and expensive. No one in his village owned one. Only a few wealthy people could afford them in the province of New Mexico.

He sat up and gulped for air. The heat from the hearth stones had warmed the ledge where he slept. His night clothes clung to clammy skin. Then an idea sprouted like a bean seed. What if I could learn to make a pot? Maybe Clay Woman could teach me in return for clay from our field. I don't know how much longer the patch will hold or until the pot breaks altogether.

He climbed down, slipped on his moccasins, and tiptoed around the dry grass-filled mattress on the floor where his aunt slept. Outside, the desert air felt cool and the full moon burned bright. A skinwalker's moon. Everyone knew they came out during a full moon. Were they half man, half beast, as los vecinos believed? No one had ever seen one. It was very bad luck if you did.

To be safe, he grabbed a bow and a flint-tipped arrow, for that was the only way to kill one. And the crucifix on the rosary around his neck would help keep them away.

The boom of drum-like rolling thunder drifted from where Fools Crow lived in the old *jacal*, a small pole-and-mud hut on the other side of the hill. The beat mixed in with the song of cicadas. The medicine man must be calling forth spirits, asking for rain.

Raymundo walked the moonlit path to the field, tightly clutching the crucifix on the rosary. At once, he saw that someone had taken clay from the pit. He dropped his bow and arrow, and quickly filled his pouch. The rattle of dead leaves startled him. A movement caught his eye as a gray shadow glided across the path behind him. Raymundo held onto the pouch and ran, kicking up moonlight dust in his wake. Were those padded footfalls close behind? He dared not look. Looking at a skinwalker risked danger for himself, his family, even his village.

A sharp rock jutting from the path tore his moccasin and grazed the sole of his foot. It threw him off-balance, and he fell. He released the pouch too late to protect his head and hit a large boulder, hard. Stunned, he rolled on his back and tried to raise his head. The pain was as sharp as the thorny spikes on the *chico* shrubs lining the path. Fear propelled him. Raymundo sat up and put his hand where it hurt, on his temple. Blood ran in rivulets through his fingers, soaking his shirt. He crawled through the shrubs, the spikes scraping the skin off his arms like the claws of an angry cat. Trembling, he waited. If only he had the bow and arrow.

Raymundo huddled in fright, afraid it was the genízara, Clay Woman, who had changed shape and come after him. Did she know he had followed her to the arroyo with her secret clay bed?

A twig snapped. He sucked in his breath. An offensive smell stung his nostrils. Something stood in front of the shrub where he hid. Should he run? Too late. The limbs began to part. He froze like prey.

Terror pushed him into a void of darkness where he knew nothing could hurt him.

Raymundo went in and out of what seemed like a bad dream. Everything was fuzzy and unreal. A grotesque coyote head swayed above him like a wisp of wood smoke. The pungent smell of sage and the sound of jingles and rattles jolted him. He reached up with his hand but nothing was there.

The only thing real was the pain.

27

A presence hovered over him. And then he was swallowing a bitter, warm liquid. The strange waking dream gradually faded to the celestial song of a flute, connecting him to what must be heaven.

A vicious headache woke him up. It was cold on the ground. Raymundo slowly stood up. He felt the gash on his temple. It had stopped bleeding. The tips of his fingers came away from his wound greasy, feeling like he had touched animal fat.

The gray light changed to a bluish hue as the sun inched over the top of the eastern mountains. He leaned and picked up the pouch of clay. If he hurried, his mother and aunt would still be asleep.

Raymundo hid the clay pouch in the wood pile and had a fire going when Mamá and Tía Clotilde awoke. He wore Papá's hat to hide the wound and donned another long-sleeved shirt. The bloodied one he stuffed under his pillow until he could find a way to repair the rips and clean it.

Tuning out Tía Clotilde, he moved about the room. Every now and then he said, "Uh huh," or shook his head in response. He was eager to know what happened to him, yet terribly afraid. Was it Clay Woman? he wondered again. She was a stout, old woman, but he imagined shapeshifting would make her strong and agile.

Raymundo went back and forth trying to make sense of it all. Had he surprised her and that's why she came after him?

Where had she taken him and why wasn't he dead? Maybe she witched him like Padre Ordóñez, and a painful death would follow. But his head was doctored and he felt fine.

At the well, he dropped the bucket in while his thoughts rushed on. Should he risk going back to Clay Woman's to find out if she was the thief? That would also make her the skinwalker, if that is what chased him last night.

"Can I have the bucket?" a vecino asked.

Raymundo was staring down the well and realized he hadn't pulled the bucket back up. "Yes, here," he said, pulling on the rope. He emptied the water into his jar. As he walked, the sloshing water seemed to chant, "What shall I do? What shall I do?" So he asked Papá, already knowing the answer. He would have to put his fear aside. The family needed a bean pot.

He delivered the water to Tía Clotilde, then stuck Papá's knife in its sheath and hid it in the folds of the cloth woodsling. Off he went to the genízaro village to look for signs of reddish-brown clay.

Raymundo saw another woman working with clay today. He peered into Clay Woman's patio. A lump of gray clay was on her grinding stone. Sacks of yellow and white clay lay next to it. He could see no other clay.

Clay Woman came into view. She walked toward steaming pots on a grill. Flies buzzed around the purple-flowered bee plants in the basket she held in the crook of her arm. She dropped the flowers and stalks of each plant into the pots, and

30

set the basket down. Reaching into a cooled pot, she shaped small black cakes from its contents.

Taking an old rag, she cleaned the dust off the surface of another white pot, making it ready to decorate. She measured where to paint the design with her fingers, placing marks with her nails.

Raymundo watched as she added water to a black cake, dipped her yucca brush, and painted feathered cloud and lightning symbols, while the boy he saw yesterday shooed away flies. She plucked a fly stuck to the paint, and finished painting corn stalks along the base.

It was getting late, and Raymundo had to go. If it wasn't Clay Woman, then who was taking clay? He had to know. Only then would he feel safe enough to approach her about making a bean pot.

Five
Fools Crow

Raymundo spent the rest of the day at the bean field. He dug out the little trenches around his plants to hold more water. Toward evening, he stuck the knife in the waistband of his pants and lay on a bed of dry grasses among shriveled willows near the clay pit. He waited, watching for someone to come by. Could it be Juan? What was he telling the others about Clay Woman by the well two nights ago? He could be planning to accuse her of stealing clay.

In the quiet of day, he heard drumming like the drill of a woodpecker. Sometimes Fools Crow drummed until the early morning hours. The beat was hypnotic. Raymundo's thoughts drifted away.

An eerie sound broke through his reverie. He listened. It was the scritch-scratch of digging. Crouching, he picked his way through brush. What am I doing? This time, I may not be so lucky. He stopped. It's getting dark. Mamá and Tía Clotilde will be worried sick. If I can just get a glimpse of who it is. . . .

But the crackling of dry vegetation gave him away, and the digging stopped. He heard growling, like a sheep dog who senses an intruder near his flock.

He swiveled on the balls of his feet and yelped. A thorn poked through the tear in his moccasin. He'd forgotten to ask Juan to mend it. He limped along like a hobbled horse, when a silent, dark-winged form swooped over his head. Whoosh! Whoosh! Whoosh! *Un tecolote!* He watched the owl fly to the grove of dense cottonwood trees. The river *bosque* was known as the gathering place of witches.

"Raymundo-o-o-o-o!" They were looking for him. Firelight from torches bobbed down the hill on the path.

"I'm over here," he shouted.

Tía Clotilde and three men circled Raymundo with their torches. His aunt reached out and touched the side of his forehead. She rubbed her finger tips back and forth and held them up to the light. Blood. The hat must have rubbed off the scab.

"You're hurt! What happened?" she demanded.

He took off his moccasin and showed her the tear. "I stepped on a sharp rock sticking out of the path. I fell and bumped my head. And then my head hurt, so I lay down. I must have fallen asleep. I woke up when I heard you calling." He hated to lie.

"Fortunately, your mother is asleep and won't have to hear about this tonight."

Raymundo had managed to calm Mamá by mid-morning the next day "I'll be more careful," he promised.

Now he needed his moccasin repaired. He knocked on Juan's door. The dog growled. Could this be what he heard last night?

"He won't hurt you," said Juan, opening the door and picking up the dog. "How may I help you?"

He slipped off his moccasin. "As you can see, I am in need of a mending. I can bring a load of firewood in payment."

"Yes, of course. Let me get my tools. Can you wait?"

"I can," he replied. A good opportunity to look inside Juan's house for clay. And later, when he brought the load of wood, he could look around outside.

While Juan worked, Raymundo stooped to pet the dog, his eyes darting to every corner of the room. He straightened and looked in a woven basket hanging from a hook in the wall. He saw nothing that looked like clay.

"Here, I'm finished."

Raymundo inspected the moccasin and put it on. "Muchas gracias, Señor. I will have your wood by this evening." This would get him out of the house later.

Did he dare go out alone again tonight? Feeling desperate about the crumbling clay on the bean pot, he knew he would.

"If I am not home by nightfall, do not worry," he said to Mamá and Tía Clotilde after supper. "I will be working at vecino Juan's chopping and stacking a load of wood to pay for my moccasin."

It was late evening. He would have to hurry so that he could find a place to hide before the thief showed up at the bean field, if he came at all. He chopped a load of wood from his pile and delivered it to Juan.

This time, Raymundo came prepared. He had stowed his bow and two arrows inside the adobe oven after supper. At the field, he waited where he would have perfect aim to drive an arrow through the heart of a skinwalker.

Tonight, he would know who it was, for he could see clearly with the light of the harvest moon. As he waited, he felt a sadness for how it was when Papá was alive. During harvest, all the vecinos got together in celebration. First, they attended mass to thank San Ysidro, the saint who takes care of farmers and their crops. Then the women harvested the bean crop, and the men harvested the corn and grain. When the work was done, they gathered for a fiesta with music and dancing. But because of the drought, it was unlikely there would be much of a harvest this fall, and it wouldn't be the same without Papá even if there were.

The longer he waited, the harder it was to stay calm. He picked at the scab on his forehead. He fidgeted with the sinew bowstring, making sure it was tight. He kicked at the dirt on the ground. Just then, a creature appeared at the site. It had the head of a coyote and animal hair running down the back.

Raymundo gasped. Trembling, he fumbled with the bow and arrow, pulled on the bowstring, and took aim. The creature knelt. Raymundo saw that the legs were human, as were the hands digging clay. A drop of blood clouded his eye, and the arrow flew before he was ready. Swissssh. It fell short of its mark. The creature jerked its head in his direction.

He should have run, but there was something familiar about what Raymundo saw. With a menacing growl, the creature rushed at him. Raymundo wouldn't scare this time. Instead, he stood his ground. "So you are the thief, Fools Crow."

Fools Crow halted in midstride. "You know my name?"

"I know who you are. Why do you steal my clay?"

"It is not for me that I do it." He backed away.

"It is wrong to steal either way. But tell me, who do you do it for?"

"Clay Woman, the pot maker. She feeds me when I am hungry. No one else will." His twisted body seemed to be wasting away.

"Why don't you live with the others?"

"I stand accused of inflicting bad spirits on my village."

His own people think he is a sorcerer. And Clay Woman, do they also think she is a witch?

"It was you who helped me the night of the full moon, wasn't it?"

"I had asked for a good hunt that night, but the evil spirit kills everything with its fiery breath. I only meant to frighten you."

"You took me to your home?"

Fools Crow pointed. "Yes, on the other side of the hill."

"Have you given clay to Clay Woman?"

"No, I carry only a small amount each time. Soon I will have enough. She is getting old, too old to go far for clay. There is plenty here, and no one to use it."

"You could have asked for some."

"I was afraid."

Then Raymundo said, "I, too, know of Clay Woman and her pots. And I wish to give her clay myself, in return for teaching me to make a bean pot, but I fear she will refuse."

Fools Crow didn't hesitate. "I will speak in your behalf."

Satisfied, Raymundo said, "Keep the clay, then. I will take her some tomorrow."

Six

A Leap of Faith

Arriving early, Raymundo stayed behind the chamiso until he gained the courage to talk to Clay Woman. She seemed unaware that he was there, but like the owl, Clay Woman seemed to see what others could not. He jumped like the long-legged jackrabbit when she spoke. "What brings you here?" she asked.

"I-I ha-have b-b-brought you clay." Had Fools Crow forgotten to speak to her? Should he have trusted the old fool? Losing confidence, Raymundo's hand shook when he slipped the pouch through a gap in the poles of the fence.

"Clay?" she said and reached for the pouch.

"There is more. In my bean field," blurted Raymundo. "Will you teach me to make a bean pot in return for clay?"

"You . . . make a pot?" She studied him.

"Soon, we will have nothing to cook in. Our pot is old and cracked."

Clay Woman ground a small amount and added water.

Then she coiled the mud-like clay around her finger. It was smooth as snakeskin and showed only tiny cracks.

She looked up. "Genízaros are not allowed on Spanish land."

"It is my family's land. You will be safe with me." He prayed no one would see them.

She took her time to respond. "Tomorrow then when the rooster crows, show me."

"I will be here," said Raymundo. He left before she changed her mind.

That night, he could not fall sleep. What if she *was* a witch? And put a hex on him—or worse. All his life he had been taught to fear the genízaro witches. He turned to prayer as always. I will put my faith in you, Saint Anthony, he prayed.

Still, he tossed and turned most of the night. Towards dawn, he slept. Too soon, the rooster crowed.

Qi-qirri-qi-qi! Qi-qirri-qi-qi! Raymundo jumped out of bed fully dressed.

Clay Woman waited at the fence, digging stick and cloth sack in hand. Raymundo muttered a quick buenos días and walked ahead. Occasionally, he'd slow down a bit so that she could catch up.

The sun's rays had painted the sky in shades of red and pink when they reached the bean field, which was much closer than Clay Woman's clay bed. This should make her happy.

Clay Woman knelt. She used a digging stick to break off chunks of reddish-brown clay with mica flakes that glittered in

43

the sunlight. Her face also gleamed like a treasure of Spanish doubloons.

Raymundo stared in awe at the gold-colored mica. He hadn't noticed it before.

"Thank you, Old Clay Mother, for this bed of rich clay," she prayed. "May it hold the gift for pot making."

She prays to a saint, like I pray to Saint Anthony? Raymundo looked at her in surprise. A smile played on her lips, a smile that melted away his fear. He smiled back.

"Now, the clay must pass some tests," Clay Woman said.

What did she mean by this? Was it not good clay? Already in a hurry for a bean pot, he wondered how long it would take.

Clay Woman filled the cloth sack and lugged it to her patio. Raymundo followed.

She sifted the clay through a reed-woven basket to get rid of pebbles and twigs. Raymundo watched. Then she sat at one of the metates and worked the stone *mano* to grind it. Again, he watched. She stopped grinding and remained seated on the ground, unmoving, her head bowed.

Raymundo took the water jar and placed it in front of her. Her hand shook slightly as she reached for it. The water seemed to revive her.

"May I?" he said. She handed him the jar. He took a drink of fresh water, tastier than any he'd had in a long time.

She continued grinding clay until it was fine powder. "Next, I mix in grog, and only then will we know if your clay is good for making pots," she said. "For this, I need pieces of broken pots, but I have only a few. I can no longer climb the mesas in search of shards left there by the ancestors."

"My neighbors, los vecinos, have many," said Raymundo. "Tomorrow, I will bring shards, but now I must go." He would bring the shards first thing in the morning, so there would be no more delay. He had thought they would be making pots today.

A longing to be with Papá ached within, as he searched for wood in the foothills. Being with Clay Woman today made him miss Papá more than ever.

Raymundo talked to him to take the edge off the pain.

"If I hurry and gather wood, Papá, I will have time to care for my bean plants, *and* ask los vecinos for shards before bedtime. I hope they are feeling generous."

He stooped and picked up a stick. "I can hardly wait for tomorrow to see if my clay works for making pots."

Then the excitement waned and a desperate wanting filled him. "But only one thing would make me happier, Papá. If only I could see you again." Tears stung his eyes, threatening to fall. He yanked the hat off and rubbed his sweaty head. What good would crying do?

Raymundo came to a downed tree. Tired, he set his woodsling on it, sat down, and stared off into the distance.

It felt hotter than ever. How long had it been since it rained? The thunderheads over the mountains would not make it this far again today. And every day, it seemed Raymundo had farther to go to find firewood.

He took the last drink from his skin bag. Then he gathered a large load to replace what he gave Juan, and went home to drop it off. His arms ached; beads of sweat gathered on his temples and ran down his back. Tía Clotilde wiped his face with a handkerchief she kept tucked in her long sleeve and lifted the wood-sling off his shoulder. "Such a large load to carry," she said, helping him stack it by the house. She loaded his arms with wood and followed, carrying a few sticks herself.

Raymundo set the wood by the hearth. "I'll be back before dark," he said to Tía Clotilde and Mamá.

"Don't make us come looking for you again. Your mother cannot take the worry," added Tía Clotilde. Then she issued a warning. "And vecina Ana says witches do their evil work at night."

The water in the ditch was muddier now, barely flowing. Still, Raymundo took what he could in his jar and watered each plant, trudging back and forth, back and forth in the blinding heat. And he worried about what he would say when he asked los vecinos for shards tomorrow, since watering took longer than he'd planned.

He couldn't tell them he needed the shards to make a bean pot.

Seven
The Betrayal

The next morning, Raymundo stuck his hand under his pillow and pulled out the little casket where he kept the silver milagros. He put one in his pocket. Then he practiced what he would say to los vecinos. "May I have a shard or two to grind and fertilize my bean plants?" he asked neighbor after neighbor. Again, he lied. Tonight, he would ask Saint Anthony to forgive him. And when the priest came again, he would go to confession.

"I will surprise everyone with a new bean pot," he said to Papá on the way to Clay Woman's, since he had gathered enough shards to make pots for everyone. He saw in the glittering clay the possibility of finished pots. In it, he also saw Mamá cooking a pot of new-crop beans.

At Clay Woman's he plopped his bundle of shards next to the metate and sat under the tree. He heard a dog bark. A boy from his village walked past with two bedraggled sheep. Raymundo scrambled to hide behind the cottonwood until the sheepherder was gone.

Clay Woman looked up when Raymundo came out from behind the tree. He avoided looking at her. Without a word, she sat with a sharpened piece of wood and carved a design into the moist clay of a gray pot. She painted symbols for water—fish, tadpoles, a flowing river. "I ask for a blessing," she said.

Raymundo nodded. He sent out his own prayer. Maybe now it would rain.

Clay Woman continued working on her pot. As the time passed, he realized she wasn't going to work with him.

"I will come again tomorrow?" he finally said. He had so much to do.

Clay Woman looked deep into his eyes. "Yes, come, but only if it is in your heart."

What she said puzzled him. Of course it was in his heart to come. He needed a bean pot, didn't he?

Raymundo stopped to check his bean plants. A cloud of dust arose in the distance, sending his heart racing. Comanches! Run, run, his mind screamed. He ran up the hill, desperate to make it to the plaza where los vecinos barricaded themselves from attack. As he ran, he looked over his shoulder and saw it was a large dust devil, larger than he'd ever seen before, towering as high as a cottonwood tree. The hotter it got, the larger the dust devils. He bent over his knees to catch his breath, and waited for his side to stop aching. On his way,

he stopped at a neighbor's to trade a silver milagro for a skin of goat's milk.

Raymundo took a bite of the meal Tía Clotilde prepared in the bean pot. He spit it out. Crumbs of clay had peppered their food. The patch was slowly wearing away.

"Ay, Jesús Cristo," cried Tía Clotilde, wiping her mouth on her stained apron. "What could be worse than this?"

"Hardly anyone has pots left," said Mamá in little more than a whisper. She set her bowl down.

Raymundo smoothed her blanket. "God will provide," he said, and gave her a few drinks of fresh goat's milk. Before Mamá fell asleep, they prayed for the intercession of his favorite *santo*, Saint Anthony, as they did every night.

He went to bed after he patched the pot again. The crack had grown twice as large as before.

Visions of pots he would make crowded Raymundo's dreams, but Mamá's moaning is what woke him up. He dangled his feet off the hearth ledge and pushed off with his hands.

"What is it, Mamá? "Raymundo touched her skin. She was burning up, delirious with fever.

"Witch . . . evil eye . . . ," mumbled Mamá, tossing and turning, clutching her stomach.

"Ah, then it is so. The old genízara crone *has* witched her," said Tía Clotilde, her long gray hair flying, looking very much like a crone herself.

"No, Tía. Something has made her sick " He didn't want to believe Mamá had been witched. Not by Clay Woman.

Tía Clotilde yanked a large gourd off the shelf. "Go, fill this with water. Then build a fire. *¡Aprisa!*" Raymundo ran to the well to draw water.

While Tía placed cold rags on Mamá's forehead, Raymundo built a small fire in the hearth to boil *álamo*, the wild herb for stomach pain. With every passing second, he feared her stomach would distend like a bloated cow's, and her nose would bleed out all her blood from swollen veins.

The medicine calmed Mamá, and she slipped into fitful slumber.

Tía Clotilde looked exhausted. Raymundo helped her to bed, and she fell asleep right away.

Then he dropped to the floor next to Mamá's bed, wanting to be at her side if her condition worsened. Anger welled up inside when he looked at Saint Anthony on the mantle. Standing, he grabbed the wooden carving and spun the saint around to face the wall. It toppled to the floor. "I counted on you," he whispered, not bothering to pick it up. Now Mamá was sick, and he still didn't have a bean pot. He felt a tremendous loss of faith, his despair reminding him of the sufferings on earth that Padre Sanchez preached about. Weary, his eyelids drooped, and he lay his head down.

Tía Clotilde shook him. A narrow light beam spilled in the room through the sheepskin parchment on the tiny window high on the wall. "We need a fire," she said softly. He sat up on the cold dirt floor, chilled and achy.

 51

Tía Clotilde picked up the carved saint. She looked at Mamá and dabbed her eyes with the handkerchief. "They say when a saint falls it is a sign that someone in the family is going to die." Raymundo took the saint from her and placed it back on the ledge facing the wall. He didn't want to look at Saint Anthony's face. "It was my fault it fell. No one is going to die."

The saint had no power at all.

He built a fire and then went out to the well. Today, a vecino stood guard. "The well water is dangerously low," he said, "only half a gourd."

"That is hardly enough drinking water for a family of three," said Raymundo. "And what about cooking?"

"Bring what you can from the acequia."

"The ditch is mostly mud," said Raymundo. "And Mamá is sick. We need some for her."

"There is talk she has been witched," said the neighbor.

A sharp pain tightened Raymundo's gut. Someone's been talking! He stumbled into the house. Was it Tía Clotilde?

He stayed at Mamá's side for four days, doing his chores when she slept, worrying about her, and wondering if Clay Woman was safe. What would los vecinos do to a witch? He was afraid to find out.

Mamá's fever broke that night, but word came that vecino Juan's daughter and two other neighbors had fallen sick. The talk swirling around all day was, once again, that the genízara witch had cast a deadly spell on their village.

This time, she would not get away with it.

Eight
The Dreamer and the Dream

The next day, Mamá ate spoonfuls of gruel boiled in a small amount of water. While Tía Clotilde cared for her, Raymundo sneaked away to Clay Woman's. Should he tell her what los vecinos were saying? It would mean going against them.

He showed up at her patio ready to make a bean pot like they'd agreed, if she wanted some of his clay. But would she now think it was not in his heart to make a pot, since he had stayed away so long?

Raymundo yanked open the pole gate and dropped it on the ground. He waited and waited under the cottonwood tree. Her yard was like she always left it, ready for the next day's work, but Clay Woman wasn't working today. He fastened the gate and walked home. He'd come back first thing tomorrow and pray nothing bad would happen meantime.

At home, he did his chores, helped with Mamá, and asked a few questions of those he thought might know if trouble was brewing, but no one was talking. What if it wasn't witchcraft that made people sick this time, he said. They couldn't prove it was Clay Woman.

The response was not good. Such was their belief in witches.

The noisy, early morning birds woke him. He hurried and dressed, knowing Clay Woman would be there today.

She wasn't.

He wanted to ask where she was, but the genízaros ignored him as if he were invisible, a sign of disapproval for coming here, he supposed. They seemed to tolerate Clay Woman in spite of her maverick ways. Probably because they needed her pots, but it was obvious they didn't approve of her helping Raymundo make them.

The day seemed to last forever. Raymundo split wood, watered his plants, and carried home two jars of water from the ditch. In the cool of the evening, he looked for wild berries. The *champe*, or rose hip bushes, had lost most of their leaves, and the wrinkled berries were full of worms. He picked some anyway. The boiled skins would add flavor to Mamá's gruel.

A few days went by, and every morning he looked for Clay Woman. Today, he waited outside the fence until the rooster crowed and the sun rose, but his heart sank deeper and deeper. There was no sign of her. Then he recalled the day Juan was talking to los vecinos by the well. A sliver of fear made him shiver. I'll ask Fools Crow what he knows, he decided.

The tiny jacal sat in front of a low, rocky ridge that grew sparse shrubs. The hut was built like their fences, with mud in between to fill the cracks. The old medicine man sat outside on a log. In his hand rested a shallow pottery shard with several dead crickets, which he popped in his mouth and ate without flinching. Two dead lizards baked in the sun on a rock. Bunches of withered plants with dry, empty tubers were scattered around.

Fools Crow didn't seem surprised to see Raymundo. "Have you come about Clay Woman?" he asked, belching loudly. His ribs stood out more than ever.

"Can you tell me where she is? I have been by to make pots like we agreed, and she is not there again today."

"I, too, have been there. The others, they do not talk to me." Raymundo left knowing no more than when he came.

He went back to Clay Woman's village. He knocked on a door. No answer. The others closed their doors when they saw him coming. His fear grew. Tonight he would turn the statue around and pray like never before.

Raymundo found himself on the path to her house at first light. He had to know if she was all right. And he couldn't wait anymore for a pot. He sat outside the gate and rested his head on his knees. He felt responsible for not telling her about the dangerous rumors and would never forgive himself if something bad had happened to her.

"So, you have come." Clay Woman walked the path to the gate.

Raymundo jerked his head up. She looked thinner, her facial lines deeper, like dried-out leathery clay.

He stood and followed her to the door of her hut. She set her traveling bundle inside.

"Clay Woman! I . . . I thought . . . you. . . . Mamá was sick. . . ." Then, "I came to warn you," he cried. "The vecinos are saying horrible things, and I am afraid of what they might do."

He paced. "They are accusing you of witchcraft and of placing a curse on our village again. Mamá and three others are sick, and they blame you. I, too, believed you might be a witch, but now I don't think you are."

Clay Woman looked at him, and he stopped pacing. "I have been accused before," she said. It was clear she was unafraid.

Fools Crow walked up with a small load of wood. He and Clay Woman spoke in their language. Raymundo felt dismissed. He stood by the metate where the shards and powdered clay were.

"Will we make pots today?" he asked Clay Woman.

Clay Woman looked away. "You are not ready," she replied. She sat on her goat skin to work on a pot and didn't speak again.

Raymundo's disappointment hung heavy between them. Clay Woman appeared not to notice. Did she not know he took a risk coming here to warn her? And what about clay? She could have all she needs. He walked out the gate and down the path. She must have changed her mind about helping him.

His hopes dashed, he squeezed his head with his hands. What am I going to do now?

Someone tapped his shoulder. He turned around and bumped into Fools Crow.

"What do you want?" snapped Raymundo.

"I come to offer help."

"How can you help me? Do you know why Clay Woman says I am not ready?"

"There is something you should know."

"I don't know what you mean."

"Meet me later. Only then can I show you."

This scared him. He was afraid of Fools Crow's strange ways. But Raymundo agreed to go. I have nothing to lose, he thought. He did help me once before when I was hurt. Then he remembered the snake incident and his fear returned.

He arrived at Fools Crow's *jacal* at mid-afternoon. The old man was waiting. With the leather bag on his shoulder, Fools Crow led him away to a canyon. They climbed its slope until they came to an outcropping. He watched Fools Crow disappear behind a large boulder. Now was Raymundo's chance to get away. Instead, he followed and found him lighting a torch.

Fools Crow's sacred cave was small and musty. Even though the Spaniards had wanted all traces of the genízaros' religion swept from their village, Fools Crow continued to practice in the old way.

He built a small fire, which gave more light than the torch alone. There was a drum, a rattle, and other objects on a rock

shelf, and an animal skin on the ground. Raymundo was instructed to lie down. He did as he was told.

"I remove a blockage," said Fools Crow. "Only then will your answer be revealed." He sat next to Raymundo and started to drum a heartbeat rhythm. Raymundo drifted into the waking dream he had experienced before, but remained more alert. When the drumming stopped, the sound of a rattle took over, which had the same hypnotic effect.

Fools Crow was kneeling, shaking the rattle over him and praying. Raymundo eyelids grew heavy, and he closed his eyes. They flew open when he heard a second voice joining in prayer, the words echoing off the walls. The sharp whispers were that of an old woman.

Something about being in Fools Crow's presence seemed to make Raymundo see and hear things that weren't there.

Without warning, he leaned over Raymundo's chest, made a sucking sound and spit into a basket with sand. Fools Crow continued to make the sucking sound again and again, each time spitting into the basket. "There, it's gone," he said at last. "Now I sing a power song for your protection," and he began to chant.

Within minutes, it was over, but Raymundo knew he had experienced something spiritual and powerful. A soothing comfort followed, similar to going to church on Sunday or praying to Saint Anthony, and he just wanted to lie there.

Fools Crow said, "Come, your answer will be revealed sooner or later. But you must listen and see."

As they left the cave, Raymundo still felt lightheaded and had to watch his step.

For days, Raymundo wondered how and when his answer would come, or if it would come at all. Would it be like an answer to a prayer, or a small miracle?

It came in the most unusual way.

Raymundo was sound asleep, tired from the day's work. He started to dream, but this was no ordinary dream. The difference was that he knew he was dreaming. He couldn't see himself but knew he was seen, because Clay Woman walked by and waved to him. She was at her clay bed. Through her, he saw the story of pot making unfold step by step. She lovingly dug her clay, cleaned it, ground and soaked it, kneaded, molded, and baked it. The mother, tending to her child from birth to womanhood—from raw clay to beautiful pot.

Raymundo recalled the dream when he awoke, and with simple information, it foretold his future. He knew what to do.

Raymundo took a digging stick and the empty sacks from Clay Woman's yard, and filled them with clay at the bean field. He dragged and carried and rolled them back to her patio. He poured a little clay at a time into the basket, sifted it clean like he'd seen Clay Woman do, and then sat on the ground in front of the metate to grind it. "Take your time, Raymundo, and do it right," he heard Papá say when he got in a hurry. He ground it twice to get the fine powder Clay Woman wanted.

Raymundo's muscles ached. He lowered his head to rest, rubbing his arms. A shadow loomed overhead and startled him. He looked up. Clay Woman.

"I see you are ready," she said.

"Yes," he replied.

Together they ground more shards and clay and put the powder into jars of water to soak. Then they poured off the water and set the moist clay on flat stones. Raymundo helped knead the mixture like Mamá kneaded tortilla dough. Tía Clotilde would throw a fit if she knew. "The man of the house does women's work?" she would say. Her gossip would spread like butter on a hot tortilla, far beyond the village gates.

Next, Clay Woman divided the kneaded batch of clay into large chunks and covered it with a moist cloth, allowing it to cure overnight and become more workable for shaping pots.

Nine
Song of the Singing Stones

Raymundo came early and joined Clay Woman on the goat skin.

She prayed, "Ancestors, guide our fingers as we make this clay into many good pots."

Next, she set a puki mold to form the base of the pots on a slab of wood in front of Raymundo. She sprinkled the inside with fine ashes so the wet clay would not stick. Taking a flat cake of clay, she showed him how to press it against the mold. Raymundo followed her instructions with ease.

A tingling energy filled the air as he pounded and kneaded, coiled and pinched, scraped and smoothed the glittering clay. Earthen colors and smells surrounded him. A breeze stirred, and the singing stones hanging from a branch on the cottonwood sang clear and sweet—like the song in his heart.

Clay Woman's magic is not of hexes and evil deeds, thought Raymundo, but he was spellbound just the same. If only he could tell los vecinos, they would see her as he did.

"Clay is a living thing," said Clay Woman. "Talk to it, listen to its voice, for it tells you what shape it wants to be."

Raymundo believed he'd heard the clay's voice. By mid-morning, he had shaped three bean pots with rims and handles. His clay had passed another test. If time allowed, he would make three more and polish them all before noon.

When Raymundo finished making the rest of his pots, he sat in the shade of the tree to polish them, but even there it was hot. He reached into his pocket for the river stone. Clay Woman took three more stones from her pouch. She showed him how to rub them back and forth, smoothing and polishing the surface of the pots to a pearly sheen with a mica-flecked glitter. He polished, forgetting the time. His fingers ached from rubbing, his throat from thirst. He stood, stretched his legs, and walked behind the tree. Clay Woman's water jar was full again.

Peering around the tree, he asked, "May I have a drink?" Clay Woman nodded.

Where is the fresh water coming from? he wondered, taking a long drink. The wells were almost dry. Everyone in his village was getting water from wherever they could. He felt the sting of guilt as he tipped the jar again. He wiped his lips with the back of his hand, then poured a few drinks in his water skin to take to Mamá. Did he dare ask Clay Woman where she got the water? He didn't know if he should. What if she wasn't supposed to tell?

There was plenty of water for Clay Woman to mix clay paint. Raymundo stood quietly by to learn how. When the paint was ready, he polished the last two pots and coated the inside of each one with brown paint using a small mop made of cloth, like the one she had used when he'd watched the first day. He applied a narrow red band on the outside rim with a yucca brush.

As he waited for the clay paint to dry, Raymundo chewed slender leaves of yucca to make more brushes, savoring the sweet flavor of the juice as it soothed his chapped lips. He basked in the silence of Clay Woman's world, so different from his home life with his babbling aunt.

Then Clay Woman handed Raymundo a basket. He went with her to the woods to collect the sacred plants for dyes, which they found were brown and useless. They gathered lichen instead, small flowerless plants forming a crust on rocks and trees. At the foothills, they collected juniper berries and wild cherry root.

"Color begins with light and comes from the earth, as we came from the earth," said Clay Woman. "It is all around, in the red and purple sunset, the brown of tobacco, the green of plants and leaves."

She held out a handful of juniper berries. "I use certain colors to show things," she explained. "To some, white is pure and black a place of darkness."

Colors are like people, Raymundo mused. We see each other as good or bad.

"Color can bring a blessing," she told him, "as in a rainbow after a rain, where colors touch and together create a whole."

He thought about this on the way back to her patio.

65

Clay Woman had him carry a jar of water to the grill to mix dyes. She dropped lichen, juniper berries, roots, and ground-up pebbles in pots of boiling water to render different colors. He watched her strain the dyes through cloth: yellow dye from lichen, purple from wild cherry root, and light brown from juniper.

"There is much to making dyes. In time, you will learn," she said. She looked at the polished pots. "Tomorrow we bake our pots."

Straightaway, he tackled the next task, anxious for the firing. Raymundo filled the wood-sling with dry dung chips from the horse and cattle corrals, sheep folds, and goat pens, and piled them by the fire pit. Again, he hurried home excited about tomorrow.

Tía Clotilde was braiding Mamá's hair when he walked into the house. "How are the beans doing in this heat, mi'hito?" asked Mamá. "Will we have a good crop at harvest?"

"We will," said Raymundo, not wanting to worry her. He kissed her forehead on his way out the door. Then he turned and blew Tía Clotilde a kiss. She giggled like a girl.

Ten

A Sign from the Angel of Death

Crossing the field to the bean patch, his moccasins crushed scorched bean plants with each step. He looked around at the amber-colored landscape, no longer the lush green of the river bottomland. With the smoldering heat came the inescapable smells—rotting animal carcasses, dead fish in foul water, stench from outhouses and unwashed bodies.

Raymundo looked into the field next to his, and a frightening image crossed his mind; two bony horses appeared to be pulling the death cart of Doña Sebastiana, Angel of Death. A bad omen. He closed his eyes to chase the image away and made a sign of the cross, reciting a prayer over and over again. He hurried to the ditch for water.

"Oh, no!" he exclaimed. The acequia held only mud.

He threw Papá's hat on the ground and kicked up a spray of dirt that landed on the small patch of beans struggling to survive. Leaves had begun to wither, turning gray on the underside. "I must get water to them," he groaned.

Raymundo would have to drop down the steep bank to the

small stream that was once a river. Soon, it too would evaporate. Until then, it would be nearly impossible to haul enough water home from the stream, taking the better part of a day to carry a jar or two, providing he didn't spill it. How would he ever have time to do everything—water and hoe his plants, collect wood and water for cooking, and make bean pots. Tomorrow, he would ask Clay Woman where she got the water to fill her jars.

Holding his clay jar close, he squatted and slid over the lip of the embankment. He stopped to rest a moment. The torrid heat kept the animals, birds, and insects hiding quietly in shade. Suddenly, a murder of crows left the trees, shattering the silence. Terror gripped him and his stomach cramped. He dropped his jar. It rolled down, down, down and landed on the rocks below. The blood-curdling war cry sent him scrambling to hide under the overhang. Peering through the fringe of dried weeds at the top, he watched Papá's hat trampled by the sharp-edged hooves of the Comanches' horses. A horse and rider crashed through his dry sagebrush fence. Raymundo's sparse crop brought a scream of outrage. The thieves came to steal what others planted, but found only field crops parched by drought.

A brave swiftly guided his horse to the edge as if he knew Raymundo was there. Frightened out of his mind, Raymundo stepped back, tumbling backward down the bank. He hit the rocks, landing on his back next to his jar. Don't move, and don't look up, he told himself. He wanted to keep his eyes

closed forever, for his worst nightmare was upon him. But he opened them to see where the Comanche brave was, and locked eyes with the man staring down at him. Raymundo knew what would come next.

An evil grin formed on the Comanche's face as he heeled his horse over the edge. Raymundo bolted to the other side of the stream and attempted to climb the bank. He was scooped up like a sack of beans and thrown over the horse's back. The wind was knocked out of his belly, a hand holding him down. The horse's canter jarred his bones, making him want to throw up.

The raiders rode away, but not before they took the neighbors' starved horses. They'd come too far to leave with nothing.

In moments, it was over. Raymundo reared upward to look back. He saw his bean field growing smaller and smaller as they headed north. Would he ever see it again? Or Mamá and Tía Clotilde?

They galloped like this until Raymundo thought he would die. His head thumped on the horse's back like his heart thumped in his chest. He could feel the horse moving beneath him, straining to keep up while the brave kicked and urged it on. After what seemed like hours, the Comanches stopped in an arroyo, which was unfamiliar to him. There were many of these gullies tucked among the foothills and mesas around here.

The brave he rode with yanked Raymundo up by the back

of his shirt, grabbed his water skin and, without removing it, drank Mamá's water. Then he shoved Raymundo to the ground next to the horses, where he was hobbled like an animal. There would be no chance for escape from his captors. And they didn't seem to care if he lived or died, since they spared no water or food for him. He was all but forgotten.

One of the stolen horses was killed with an arrow through the eye. Raymundo watched the five men cut out the liver and eat it raw. Then they carved its flesh, roasted it over a fire, and ate like scavenging predators.

Raymundo's thirst was fierce, and he would have drunk anything, even the dead horse's blood had it been offered. He raised the water skin to his mouth and tried desperately to draw water out. Then he wrung and licked it, looking for moisture.

Thirst and hunger kept him awake throughout the dark, cool night, but he didn't cry out. Instead, he sat in silence. Clay Woman said there was wisdom in silence. He prayed for an end to his misery—for he knew if he survived, the rest of his life would be lived as a Comanche slave. "I would rather die than live among these wretched horse-eaters. I ask God for mercy, for death would be better."

But he was alive in the morning. The sun came up like a ball of fire, making it the hottest drought day yet. Raymundo's fear paralyzed him, and he offered no resistance as he was lifted onto the other stolen horse. His hands were tied in front, and he leaned into the horse's neck as it was led by a rope.

73

This kept the sun from burning his face to a crisp, but the back of his neck was exposed. If only he had Papá's hat. Who knows what happened to it.

Raymundo lost all track of time. At one point, he forced himself to look ahead and saw the Comanches were suffering from the heat, too. Their horses moved slowly over the baked earth, while the men slumped lower and lower. Where were they planning to feed and water the horses? He couldn't think of any place out here in this sagebrush desert.

Raymundo grasped handfuls of mane to hold on, but his hands were getting weaker. As the sun blazed, sucking the life out of him and the horse, the horse staggered and his legs buckled, releasing the brave's hold on the rope. A horrible squeal rang out, like the squeal of a pig being butchered, and the horse fell to the ground, throwing Raymundo clear.

The Comanches barely looked back, knowing neither would last much longer anyway.

Raymundo's nightmare had just begun.

Eleven
Left in the Desert

He didn't know how long he'd been lying there on the scalding desert floor. Raymundo opened his eyes to a slit. The sun, a blazing disk, shimmered and danced in the cloudless sky. Hearing a groan, he stirred, and wished he hadn't. His body was on fire. It took a while to focus on the large bird with a red head and legs. It stared at him. This was no morning bird, and the groan was not Raymundo's. The vulture groaned again, circling.

Raymundo knew he would get his death wish now. His suffering would soon be over, but he felt a deep sadness for Mamá and Tía Clotilde and what the drought would do to them. He couldn't even cry; his tears had dried up.

"Why did you leave us, Papá?" he whispered through swollen throat and lips.

Papá's voice whispered in his heart. "Raymundo. I'm here, Raymundo."

Everything disappeared from his senses, except the sound of Papá's voice and his name being called. I must be dead, and now I'm with Papá, he thought, giddy with joy.

The vulture, smelling death, moved closer, close enough to peck at Raymundo's eye, but Raymundo saw it coming and turned his head away. The sharp beak tore his ear, and he knew he was alive. It hurt.

A strong will to live seeped into his awareness, and his raspy voice called out, "Where are you, Papá?" He rolled his head slowly, looking for him. There in the shimmering waves of heat, he saw him. Papá beckoned.

"Let's go home, mi'hito."

Raymundo tried to stand, but his shaky legs gave out each time. Finally, an unexplainable energy surged through his body and his legs held strong while he walked toward Papá, who kept walking slightly ahead.

The vulture would have to feast on the dead horse. Raymundo was going home.

He talked to his father as always, telling Papá about the Comanche raid and his trampled bean patch—while they walked, and walked, and walked. . . .

The intense glare reflecting off the desert floor blinded him. The heat swirled up from the ground causing sand and dirt to sting his sensitive skin like the bite of an army of ants. Animal skeletons were scattered like dead wood. His bones would not join them.

Raymundo shuffled and stumbled along following Papá.

Before long, they came to a small cattail oasis in the middle of nowhere. Raymundo could hardly believe what he saw. He dropped to the ground, took a drink from a small pool rimmed with alkaline, and spit out the salty water. Frantic, he tried again. Then Papá motioned for him to follow the stream to where the spring bubbled out of the ground. "*Un ojito*, Papá!" A natural spring that flowed year-round. This water he could drink, but he drank too much too fast. Some came shooting back up, running out of the sides of his mouth, choking him as he lay there squirming.

When he was able, he filled his water skin and dragged himself to the shade of a squat cedar pine. Hunger pangs wracked his body. He noticed the flutter of grasshoppers among the dried weeds next to him. The insects hopped about as he poked with a dry stick. He caught three and tore off their heads. When they were still, he put one in his mouth. It crackled like *chicharrones*, small cubes of crispy-fried pork skins with a pad of fat, but the taste was unlike anything he'd ever eaten. Tasting vomit, he gagged but forced himself to hold it down. The others were easier to eat. His hunger satisfied for now, he slept well past sunset.

When he awoke, he felt stronger but realized sadly that he could no longer see Papá.

The moon was half full, offering just enough light to see through the brush. He took the stick to help keep his balance. If a wild animal decided to attack, this would be his only protection. The barks and yaps he heard belonged to a coyote.

Coyotes were afraid of humans, usually, but Raymundo would rather not encounter a hungry one out here by himself with only a stick for a weapon.

He started off, walking in the same direction as before. The level land kept him at the base of the mesas. He stayed out of arroyos to avoid dead ends and rock walls.

The coyote howled again. This time the sound was different, almost human. You're hearing things, he scolded. To him, everything seemed different in the dark, even sound. Raymundo closed his eyes and gathered his will. He concentrated on making it home alive. He thought of his mother, how she depended on him. Would his bean plants all be dead by now? What about Clay Woman? Had los vecinos sought revenge? He needed to get back soon, thankful that Papá helped him start this journey home.

It seemed he had walked all night and lost his sense of direction. Was he walking in a circle? He was so tired, he couldn't think. His burned skin had blistered, the pain wearing on him. He listened hard for the sounds of the night to tell him where he might be. Rest, he needed to rest and regain his bearings. No, there wasn't time. He had to make it home by dawn before the sun came up again. The Comanches couldn't have traveled too far before the heat slowed them down.

He walked on like a sleepwalker.

Next thing he knew, Papá was carrying him to bed and tucking him in, just like he did every time Raymundo fell asleep before bedtime.

"Buenas noches, Papá."

Raymundo knew where he was by the smells and sounds. He'd been here before and wasn't surprised when Fools Crow walked into the jacal.

He raised himself up on his elbow. Puzzled, he asked, "How did I get here?"

"I found you while hunting. You were wandering in the prairie, alone, and near death," said the old Indian.

"Does anyone know I'm here?"

"Everyone thinks you are dead, or a captive of the Comanche."

"Poor Mamá, Tía Clotilde. And Clay Woman? Is she well?

"Yes. She prays for your return."

He stood. "How long have I been here?"

"Long enough to heal your wounds and feed your hunger."

Raymundo didn't want to know what he ate.

"You have done well healing me. I feel I can go home now." Fools Crow was a powerful medicine man. It was unfortunate that his people had accused him of wrongdoing.

Fools Crow nodded his head. "Here," he said, reaching for Raymundo's water jar.

"You found it!" A large wedge was missing from the rim.

"I have watered your plants. You worked hard so they could live."

"My plants are alive?" he said. "I will repay you for everything you've done." Fools Crow had saved his life more than once, and so much more.

"You have been kind and spared me when you could have punished me for taking clay."

Raymundo, dizzy with excitement, said farewell and took his water jar and walked to the bean field. Just like Fools Crow said, most of his plants were hanging on to life. It was a miracle any of them had survived the raid. One bean plant yielded many beans. If he, Mamá, and Tía Clotilde could survive until the rains came, finally after the harvest they would have beans to eat.

He gave out a loud whoop, snatched up a piece of driftwood, and threw it into the murky stream that flowed like the tears making tracks down his face. Now he could cry. He cried out all the anguish, and he cried tears of joy. He looked up, arms out reaching for the sky. "You hear me, Papá, when I call to you. And Saint Anthony, he has heard me, too."

When he could cry no more, he wiped his nose and eyes. Then he looked for Papá's hat. He couldn't find it anywhere.

81

Twelve
Revenge

Raymundo wanted to ask vecino Juan to break
the news of his homecoming to Mamá and Tía Clotilde, but
according to vecina Ana, he and his wife kept vigil at their
daughter's bedside. She was deathly ill.

Vecina Ana announced him instead.

Mamá held him in her arms for a long time while Tía Clotilde stood by and cried. "We had given up hope, mi'hito."

He wanted so much to tell her about Papá, how he had
helped him find his way home, but now was not the time.
Mamá had had enough excitement for one day.

In celebration, Tía Clotilde served up a bowl of *caldito*, a
broth made from a soup bone passed from family to family.
The mood was festive, and Raymundo wanted it to last forever.
He pretended he didn't notice the broth seeping through the
patched crack. Mamá and Tía Clotilde ignored it, too.

In the morning, Raymundo's atole cup remained empty. His
aunt had ground the last of the blue corn for tortillas last night.
He ignored his hunger and raced to Clay Woman's.

Fools Crow stood with her, and they were each eating a corn tortilla. Raymundo's stomach growled. She handed him a tortilla from the *comal*, a clay griddle on her grill. Then she laid a hand on Raymundo's shoulder and pointed to the pots. "I have waited for you to bake our pots."

He could hardly believe his luck. How did she know he would be back?

Clay Woman placed their pots on a stone grate. Raymundo helped cover them with dung chips.

"Here, let me," he said. She told him where to place thin flat stones over and between each pot to protect them from too much heat.

Clay Woman lit the fire. It would take all day for the smoldering dung to bake the pots. "Sometimes my pots break when they cool overnight," she said.

The final test. Raymundo could hardly wait to see if his pots had survived the chilly night.

In the cool of the next morning, Clay Woman lifted the pots carefully from the ashes with two sturdy sticks and arranged them on level ground. Only one bean pot had broken! The designs on Clay Woman's pot baked a rich black on white, and she caressed it as a mother would a child. Raymundo admired his pots that rang like a bell when he rapped them with his knuckles.

"Thank you, Clay Woman, for this wonderful gift," he said.

Clay Woman blinked from the glare of the sun. "I have given birth to a potter," she said. "Your name will be Clay Singer."

Raymundo bowed his head. "I will carry the name with honor."

"I ask but one thing," said Clay Woman.

"Anything."

"That you pass on the tradition for making clay pots."

He nodded. "I will do as you ask."

Raymundo stepped behind the tree where she kept the water jars and stooped to pick one up. It was full and heavy.

"Now, may I ask you something?"

He strained to lift the jar. Just then, he heard the whistle of an arrow hurtling through air. Thunk! The arrow whizzed by Clay Woman, who was standing in front of the pots, and struck the tree.

Raymundo dropped the jar and lunged toward her. The razor-sharp point of the second arrow tore into his upper arm, the clatter of pots breaking tore into his heart as he fell on them.

He writhed in pain. Forcing himself to his knees, he knelt on jagged shards that sliced his palms and looked at Clay Woman.

A look of confusion clouded her face as she turned toward the fence.

Raymundo followed her gaze and saw Juan. He had lowered his bow and was backing away. Two others stood with him, shouting, "Kill the witch!"

The genízaros huddled in doorways, fear etched on their faces.

"She's not a witch," cried Raymundo, struggling to stand. "Tell them, Clay Woman. Please."

Clay Woman grasped at her chest, her lips blue against an ashen face. Her raspy breath came in spurts. Gasping, her warm eyes held his for only a moment, and she crumpled to the ground.

"What have you done?" Raymundo cried, shaking his fist. "She would never hurt anyone." He fell to his knees next to her. "No! No! Nooooo! Please, don't die."

One by one, the three vecinos ran down the mesa.

"Somebody, help," he begged. "Is there anyone here that can help her?" He looked from face to face.

A woman came forward, sat, and cradled Clay Woman's head. "Fools Crow," she said.

"I will get him." Raymundo, running as nimble as a mule deer through pine, knew if anybody could save her, Fools Crow could.

Fools Crow was patching the walls of his jacal with the clay he'd gathered from the bean field.

"Come!" shouted Raymundo. "Clay Woman needs you."

The medicine man grabbed his medicine bag, and Raymundo led him by the arm at a fast pace. Once there, Fools Crow began to chant as the genízaros carried Clay Woman to her house. Raymundo held on to her hand. "Saint Anthony, we need a miracle now. Clay Woman must not die," he prayed. "There has been a terrible mistake."

Fools Crow stopped chanting at her door. He didn't allow Raymundo to enter—he wasn't genízaro.

Wiping his nose on his shirt sleeve, Raymundo stepped aside and watched until they disappeared inside. Then he picked up a broken bean pot and a shard from Clay Woman's pot and slid it in his pocket.

He would never forgive vecino Juan.

Raymundo walked home in a daze. He held the broken pot tightly in his hand, his limp arm throbbing with pain.

"*¿Que pasa*, mi'hito?" said Mamá when he came through the doorway. She looked at Raymundo's bloodied sleeve. Struggling to get out of bed, she called out, "Clotilde! Raymundo is hurt. Come quick!"

"Vecino Juan tried to kill her, Mamá." Dizzy, he staggered to the floor next to her bed, and lay his head in her lap, never letting go of the pot.

"Kill who?" she said running her hand over his hair. "Where's your tía?"

"Ay, *Dios mio*! Everybody has gone crazy," said Tía Clotilde running into the house, snorting like a horse, wiping her face with the handkerchief. "The genízara, Clay Woman, is near death. Los vecinos have accused her of witchcraft and Juan tried to kill her!"

She looked at Raymundo. "What were you doing over there?" she cried. "You could have been killed!"

Mamá looked ready to faint.

Tía Clotilde helped Raymundo stand and sat him on the wood-hewn stool by the hearth.

"Vecino Juan's daughter is very sick," said Mamá. Tears ran down her cheeks. "He blames Clay Woman."

"She taught me to make bean pots," said Raymundo. He handed Tía the broken bean pot. Tía Clotilde handled it like a piece of fine clayware. "But how? When?"

"I traded clay from our field and went to her when I could."

"They say you risked your life for her—a genízara witch," said Tía Clotilde, setting the pot down.

Raymundo winced as she cleaned his arm and wrapped it in a cloth sling. "Someone with such a good heart cannot be evil," he said. "It is because of her that we will have bean pots."

"This we keep to ourselves," Tía Clotilde said, turning to Mamá.

"What will happen between Raymundo and los vecinos now? And the genízaros? What will they do?" asked Mamá. "If only your Papá were here."

"We'll have to wait and see," said Tía Clotilde. "We don't want anyone else getting hurt, but the fear of witchcraft unfolds in strange ways."

Raymundo rose, placed the pottery shard from his pocket next to Saint Anthony, and invited Mamá and Tía Clotilde to pray—for Clay Woman's recovery and a solution to the trouble facing them all. But toward morning, vecina Ana came with the news. Clay Woman was dead, and so was Juan's daughter.

Raymundo looked for solace at his bean patch. "Why, Papá?" he asked over and over again. He began to understand that even with faith and dedicated prayer, evil still happened.

Thirteen
Whispers in the Wind

On Saturday, Raymundo awoke to the mournful toll-
ing of the mission bell. It unleashed painful memories of his
father's funeral a year ago. Two of the people he loved dearly,
gone from his life. He lit two candles and set them on the
hearth with Saint Anthony. Then he said adios to Mamá and
walked to the church.

The vecinos and genízaros were gathering inside, since
most of the genízaros now practiced the Catholic religion.
Everyone except Fools Crow. Padre Sanchez, who had arrived
from the capital late last night, greeted them all at the gate.

As Raymundo neared the church, loud wailing floated over
the high adobe wall. The Spanish women screamed in grief,
as was expected of them. When Raymundo entered, these
women dressed in black paused and gazed, and their shrieks
fell to whimpers. The mother of vecino Juan's daughter threw
herself from side to side, speaking words that made no sense,

while Tía Clotilde and the other women held her and gave her comfort.

While Raymundo stood with los vecinos on the opposite side of the church, he noticed three genízaros had hacked off their long hair to show they were mourning.

"Probably relatives," someone whispered.

The death of vecino Juan's daughter should be punishment enough for the crime against Clay Woman, thought Raymundo, looking at Juan, who appeared smaller and older than before. It seemed as if he might die of a broken heart—and Raymundo forgave him. But would Juan have to endure more punishment? Living far from the capital, the villages had no sheriff. Los vecinos and genízaros would take the law into their own hands.

Suddenly, Raymundo knew he had to do something. How could he make both sides see it was time to come together, like they came together here today? They must try to understand that what happened wasn't anyone's fault. The wrath of the drought could have caused the deaths. People were weakened by the problems it caused, leaving them unprotected from disease. He was convinced something other than witchcraft was to blame. And it was time to forgive, as Papá and Clay Woman would have wanted—for only in unity would the villages survive the death blow the drought had brought.

The priest finished the mass, and Raymundo followed the procession to the genízaros' grave site to say good-bye to Clay Woman. One man, who had been with Juan the day he tried to kill Clay Woman, spit when Raymundo walked by. Others whispered harsh words and avoided his eyes. They had not forgiven him for being at Clay Woman's that day. And he'd dared defend a genízara.

A dark force had penetrated their hearts. It had started with Juan, and the evil spread like a disease. It drove the villagers to act cold and cruel, which scared Raymundo.

The genízaros didn't stand in his way. He felt so alone at the grave after they left. The heavy wave of loss washed over him once more. "I will never forget you, my friend. Like Papá, you will remain forever in my heart."

When Raymundo left, he looked back and saw Fools Crow standing alone by the grave to say goodbye, too.

Raymundo walked to the churchyard burial ground to spend a few minutes with Papá. His heart fluttered when he opened the gate. Resting on a mound of dirt was Papá's hat. How had it gotten there? Had someone found it after the Comanche raid? Or could it be Saint Anthony answering his prayers?

He picked the hat up and spun it around and around. It was soiled and torn, but he put it on anyway, and Raymundo felt like the man he wanted to be. Like the man Papá was.

"And now, I have important work to do, Papá."

He went home and began preparations, tackling the task with renewed hope. Things would get better. People would come to their senses, the drought would be over, and Mamá's health would improve. He had to believe that.

When he asked for drinking water, it was refused. So, he went to Clay Woman's and took what was left from the spill of her jar. It would have to be enough.

Papá's small hatchet went in his waistband, the wood-sling on the shoulder opposite his wounded arm.

He traveled far in the blistering heat to the woodlands to collect fuel for baking his pots, since dung chips were even more scarce now than wood. At times, the pain was too much. The wound under the bandage felt like it had split open, but he hauled home a wood-sling laden with juniper twigs and cedar shavings in spite of it.

"Are you trying to kill yourself? What is so important that you can't rest until you heal properly," scolded Tía Clotilde as she bandaged him up again.

Raymundo fell asleep before he could answer.

Next day, instead of asking los vecinos for shards, he trudged up the distant mesa and walked in the footsteps of the ancients who had lived on its crown hundreds of years ago. There he heard their whispers in the rustle of the sage as they shared their secrets. He believed Clay Woman had joined her ancestors, and she, too, was there in spirit.

Back at home, Raymundo took Clay Woman's shard from where it lay by Saint Anthony. Then he assembled all his materials for making bean pots in his patio. Raw clay glittered in the hot sun. Pottery shards lay next to the clay. Bone scrapers, stone polishers, yucca brushes, and clay paint rested on a rug, fuel heaped at the fire pit.

He set down a frayed piece of canvas to work on. Raymundo cleaned and ground clay and shards for grog. Now, he needed water. Not only for mixing grog and clay, but for drinking and cooking, and watering his fragile plants. They would not survive another day in this heat with the small amount of water he was able to give them.

Disheartened, he rubbed Clay Woman's shard in his pocket. He pulled it out, closed his eyes, and held it in his palms. A soft breeze carried whispered words like fluffs of cotton from the trees. "*Agua*, . . . mesa." He repeated softly what he thought he heard. The clay shard had spoken as if it was Clay Woman herself.

"Yes," said Raymundo. He never got the chance to ask her where she got her water. The genízaros must have a secret source that she wants me to know about. But will they share it now, after all that's happened?

Fourteen
Clay Singer's Promise

Raymundo filled a cloth sack with clay, and got his water jar and water skin. He walked up the slope of the mesa like he had so many times to learn from Clay Woman. A thin spiral of smoke rose up to the hazy sky, toward clouds that held the promise of rain. The smell of cedar reminded him of pots baking. How he missed Clay Woman. He looked down at her people's corn fields. They were abandoned. Standing at the fence of the village, he pulled open the flimsy pole gate. The scraping noise on packed dirt screamed in the silence.

"Hola. Is anyone home?" He waited and waited. Several families lived here. Where were they?

Just then, a feeble woman came to the doorway of a stone hovel. Wide-eyed, skinny children clung to her soiled, ragged skirt.

He moved in her direction and stood next to her in the door frame where he saw people eating corn kernels floating in water, each clay bowl less than half full. He saw no other food. It was clear they were starving, for only in desperation would they eat their sacred corn seed. Even having water, they weren't strong enough to work their fields.

"My people need water," he said, handing the woman the clay sack. "Clay Woman says there is water here."

She faced the others and spoke to them for a long time. Their voices rose. They were arguing.

What he had feared must be true. They didn't want anything to do with him or his people.

Nervous, he stepped away. Now what? This had been his last hope for having water. The sun beat down on him. The raging heat reminded him of what he and all the villagers were in for. Many genízaros and Spaniards would die from the devastation of the drought. He shifted Papá's hat, pulled out Clay Woman's shard from his pocket and squeezed it tightly in his hand. He started to walk away, but a voice stopped him.

"Come, friend of Clay Woman," said an elder. He slowly led Raymundo toward the opposite end of the mesa top. They walked along the rim for a while.

The genízaros' water supply flowed from a spring that bubbled up from the ground in a grotto protected by boulders and pine. Like the one Papá led him to when he was trying to get home, only without alkaline. He flashed a thankful smile, scooped water up with his hands and drank his fill. Then he filled his jar and his water skin and hurried home. He could hardly wait to tell Mamá and the others. Surely they would forgive him now for accepting Clay Woman's generosity. Would

los vecinos also forgive the genízaros for not trading their pots and take back their accusations of witchcraft? It was a lot to hope for.

That evening, the candle on the hearth ledge flickered, sending shadows dancing along the wall that Mamá leaned on to pray. She looked stronger sitting up like this.

On the mantle were two more milagros Raymundo made when he got home—a clay image in the shape of clouds bloated with rain, and one shaped like a bean pod with seeds bursting at the seam.

He and Tía Clotilde knelt on the hard-packed dirt floor she had sprinkled and swept. Raymundo led the prayer giving thanks for the spring that filled their water jars, and asked for rain for their crops and food for their table. And forgiveness from Juan and his wife, for they still treated him with contempt. Feelings of hostility between the two villages ran deeper than Raymundo could understand.

Raymundo glanced at Mamá, who slept peacefully as he repeated the prayer for the last three beads on his rosary. "Buenas noches," he whispered.

At dawn, large cone-shaped clouds floated over the mountains and lit up like *luminarias*, festival lights on a saint's feast day. This time Raymundo knew the clouds would not melt away. His bean plants would get the needed water, and in time, the river would run again. For now, the flowing spring would supply their drinking and cooking water.

Wearing Papá's hat, he prepared for the day's work. "Send me luck, Papá."

He cleared his head and heart with prayer as he had seen Clay Woman do. "Guide me as I make my pots, Clay Woman, as your ancestors have guided you."

Then he took the shard from his pocket, ground it on the metate with the grog from yesterday, and mixed it into the ground clay. He soaked and kneaded until it was ready to mold.

Mamá and Tía Clotilde came to the patio in the afternoon. Within moments, a few curious vecinos gathered around. Some kept their distance. Before long, everyone came, except Juan and his wife.

Raymundo began to form the base of a pot using his puki. Then he made coils by pulling a rope of clay and rolling it between his hands. He laid each coil along the edge of the base and carefully pressed them into place. Using a bone scraper and watered-down clay, he smoothed the inside and outside surface as he turned and shaped the pot.

"Where did *you* learn to make pots," scoffed a vecino, "from the genízara witch?"

"Someone bring him a dress." Laughter followed.

"What good are pots when you have nothing to cook in them?" said another.

Raymundo would not give in to the taunting and cold stares he saw in the gaunt faces watching, now that Saint Anthony seemed to be hearing his prayers. "Have faith," he said. "Have I not asked for a miracle?"

He set a finished pot out to dry and faced the group. The story of Clay Woman flowed from his lips like water from the natural spring. "With forgiveness, Clay Woman's goodness can guide us," he said. "We must come together with her people and help each other through the drought."

Raymundo sensed anger build up like the dark clouds overhead.

"The genízaro and Spaniard will never unite. The differences are too great," shouted Juan, walking toward them.

"They quit trading their pots."

"Wait. Haven't Clay Woman's gifts of water and pots been a blessing?" said Tía Clotilde.

"Yes," he heard several mumble. "She's right."

"She speaks in favor of her nephew," Juan said.

Thunder boomed and got the attention of los vecinos.

They watched anxiously. Would it finally rain? Raymundo knew it would, but to him, it was as if Clay Woman held the rain at bay until he finished the last pot for the day.

Then it began to rain. A large, heavy drop here and one there, sending up tiny puffs of dust from the hot, dry ground.

Shouts of joy erupted all around. Los vecinos ran helter-skelter. Adults and children made a game of helping Raymundo cover his pots with the canvas. Everyone laughed. They gave thanks to the saint of miracles. But most importantly, Raymundo sensed that *he* had been forgiven.

And the rain poured, blessing the earth like holy water from the church font.

Fifteen
After the Harvest

The next morning, the air smelled sweet and the water-sprinkled patios were swept clean.

Mamá, Tía Clotilde, and the rest of los vecinos came again to watch Raymundo make pots, including Juan and his wife.

It rained again at the end of the day.

The rain came without fail every afternoon, and Raymundo's bean plants flourished. He had never seen such healthy plants. Hundreds of bean pods weighed the stalks down to the ground. During the warm mornings before it rained and cooled things, the pods began to turn yellow; they would need to be harvested soon.

When he wasn't at the bean field, Raymundo made pots. He could tell that a few villagers wanted to learn. They stood closer than the others to watch. One took a piece of clay and practiced making a coil.

Finally, Raymundo was ready for the firing. He felt Clay Woman's guidance, for he knew exactly where to place each pot on the stone grate for a good firing. Then he arranged the flat stones and wood around them and lit the fire.

While the pots baked, los vecinos helped Raymundo pull up bean plants and carry them home to finish drying on the tarp in the patio. The pods were already popping open. The larger stems and leaves were separated from the little bean seeds. The children walked on what was left of the stems and leaves to crush them, and the wind winnowed the rest. They harvested a nice heap of *bolita* beans, so much more than Raymundo had hoped for.

The pots baked to perfection, and everyone watched Raymundo pick each one from the ashes. The glimmering bean pots radiated a halo of golden light in the glow of the evening sun. A cheer arose. What special pots these were.

"I have made a bean pot for every family," announced Raymundo.

His neighbors lined up, and Raymundo poured a cup of dried beans into each pot ready for cooking.

"Gracias a Dios," they said in gratitude. "How can we repay you?"

"You already have," he replied, "when you accepted the gift Clay Woman gave me to make clay pots."

He turned to Mamá. "This one is for you." The radiance of Mamá's smile equaled the radiance of mica in the pots and warmed his heart. She looked happy again.

During supper, Tía Clotilde chattered like a magpie as she set out the scraps of food los vecinos had given them. "So

many beautiful pots our Raymundo has made, each one more beautiful than the next. What would we do without him? Even vecino Juan took one. Your father must be smiling down from heaven."

Raymundo could barely keep his eyes open.

"Go to sleep," whispered Tía.

This time, Raymundo fell asleep to rumblings of thunder outside, instead of rumblings from hunger like he had so many nights.

He awoke to a familiar aroma. I must be dreaming, he thought at first, opening one eye. Mamá stood without help next to the hearth, stirring beans in her new bean pot. He threw off his woven blanket and ran to her.

Raymundo feasted his eyes on the pot full of delicious beans. He picked up Mamá and spun her around, shouting, "Wake up, Tía. We have received a miracle today."

"Whaaat? Where?" And for the first time, Tía Clotilde was at a loss for words.

Raymundo looked to his santo on the hearth ledge. "I will never lose faith in you again, Saint Anthony."

The three of them sat down and ate until their stomachs were full.

A commotion drew them outside. The patio was filled with vecinos and their bean pots, along with the heavenly smell of freshly cooked beans.

Later that day, when the rain settled to a drizzle, Raymundo and his neighbors carried their bean pots up the slope of the mesa to the genízaro village.

The genízaros, along with Fools Crow, left their houses to see what los vecinos wanted, and were presented with gifts of nourishing beans.

"By sharing your water, you have saved our lives," said Raymundo. "Muchas gracias, vecinos," and for the first time he called them neighbors. He saw that rays of sunshine had pierced through clouds, and he looked for the rainbow. It glimmered brightly to the east.

A gust of wind lifted the hat off Raymundo's head. "Sí, Papá. I know you are pleased with what I have done here today, for you would have done the same."

Then the singing stones pealed their beautiful song. "I hear you, Clay Woman," and Clay Singer smiled.

The following spring, los vecinos and genízaros together dug ditches from the ojito to their fields. They celebrated an abundance of crops at harvest, more than they could eat for a long, long time.

As for Raymundo, he knew the magic of Clay Woman's love had touched them all, and it guided him in the miracle of pot making for years to come. He kept his promise to Clay Woman and passed on the ancient tradition to those who wished to learn.

And los vecinos? They made micaceous bean pots year after year, and started their own pottery tradition that lasted about one hundred years.

Their Spanish bean pots can still be found today.

Glossary

adios—goodbye

adobe—clay-like mud used for making bricks called *adobes*

acequia—irrigation ditch used for watering field crops

agua—water

álamo—cottonwood tree; medicine made from tree bark

aprisa—hurry

arroyo—brook or stream; a gully that cuts into a hill or mesa

atole—mush made from ground blue-corn flour

¡Ay, Dios mio!—My God!

barro—mud, clay

bolita—round bean; small, yellowish bean seed

bosque—woods, forest

bruja—female witch

brujo/brujos—witch (male)/witches

buenos días—good morning

buenas noches—good night

caldito—broth

Camino Real—the Royal Road to Mexico

chamiso—sagebrush

champe—rose hips; a rose hip bush

chico—greasewood shrub with sharp spikes

chicharrones—crispy, fried pork skins with a pad of fat

Chihuahua—province in Mexico

chueco—ancient game of the Pueblo people

comal—flat earthenware griddle

coyote—wolf-like animal common in North America

fiesta—a feast; party

genízara—female Christianized (Hispanicized) Indian

genízaros—Christianized (Hispanicized) Indians

Gracias a Dios—Thanks be to God

hola—hello

horno—outdoor oven made from adobe bricks

jacal—a hut

Jesús Cristo—Jesus Christ

mano—hand; smooth, round stone used to grind corn, clay, and
 other materials on the *metate*

manta—coarse cotton blanket

mesa—plateau; table-land or flat-topped hill

metate—grinding stone

mi amor—my love

mi'hito—my son

milagro—a miracle

muchas gracias—thank you very much

ojito—eye; natural spring that flows year-round

olla de barro—clay pot

padre—priest

patio—courtyard

piñon—pine tree; pine nut

plaza—adobe houses that join to form a square

pueblo—town, village; settlement

¿Que pasa?—What's up?

santo—saint; wood-carved saint

serape—type of poncho

señor—mister

sí—yes

tarima—bench

tasajos—strips of dried pumpkin

tecolote—owl

tía—aunt

tinaja—clay water jar

tortilla—flat cake made of ground wheat or corn flour

vara—unit of measurement equivalent to about three feet

vecinos—neighbors

yucca—desert plant having stiff, pointed leaves and a large cluster of white flowers

About the Author
and Illustrator

Emerita Romero-Anderson is a sixth-generation Hispana born and raised in San Luis, the oldest continuous European settlement in Colorado. Retired from teaching, she is the author of two previous books for children, *Grandpa's Tarima* and *Jose Dario Gallegos: Merchant of the Santa Fe Trail*. She lives in San Luis, where she writes and is active in community and civic work.

www.emeritaromeroanderson.com

Artist and illustrator **Randy Pijoan** is a resident of Amalia in northern New Mexico.

www.randypijoan.com